and a Sketchbook

from my Stories

STORIES FROM MY SKETCHBOOKS

and a sketchbook from my stories

BARBARA HAIGH

© Barbara Haigh 2022

Contents

Illustrations

Introduction

I first thought of writing short stories around drawings I had done in the early 1990s. I had been doing a lot of sketching in the streets of Cambridge where I lived at the time and felt that there were tales to be told triggered by these sketches. At that time I illustrated a couple of my friend Jean Blemings' short stories, and she wrote a poem about one of my drawings to which she gave the name Moon Madcap.

It was not until 2016 when my husband David saw an advert for Vicki Bertram's Writing Workshop near Kirkby Stephen in Cumbria that I decided that I would give the idea of writing a serious go. The group was very encouraging, and the tuition was at a very challenging level.

Sometimes a drawing from my lifetime's collection of sketchbooks suggested an idea for a story and sometimes the writing came first. I started a sketchbook specifically for illustrations for such stories. I found that each discipline inspired the other.

Thinking back to early schooldays we always had to draw a picture for every piece of writing, and I have found that this old idea still seems to work well for me.

I have always enjoyed illustrated books, both for children, and later for adults. The latter have fallen out of fashion but may be having a bit of a revival. I am not alone in my love of a book combining pictures and stories. Not all the writing in this book could be described as stories – some are factual pieces. Sometimes I'm not even sure which is which.

A Walk of no Consequence

The Sounds of Bob Marley

1

A Walk of no Consequence

Albert had been staring at Pete for half an hour. Pete finished his cup of tea and looked out of the window into the dark.

'Do you want to go for your walk then Albert?'

Albert looked pointedly at the hook where his lead hung – humans could be so slow on the uptake!

Pete shrugged into his old jacket. It was cold this evening and he was loth to walk the city streets, but the park would be in darkness. No street lights there. Maybe along the seafront would do.

Making sure he had his keys he pulled the door to behind him.

Mrs Mc Gee from the next door flat was just returning from her dustbin wearing a pink dressing gown with flowery pinny tightly tied round her waist and dainty velvet slippers. She hailed Pete.

'I heard your Albert barking today when you were at work. He gets lonely you know!'

'Sorry Mrs Mac. I'll be able to take him to work again tomorrow'

'He'll like that. I could always have him in with me if you're stuck,'

'Righto – thanks, see you later then.'

Pete escaped down the road to the Indian newsagent on the corner to buy some cigarettes.

'I'll have these cans of Stella while I'm about it, Ravi – and this tin of baked beans and sausages.'

'Very good Peter.'

The transaction made and paid for, Pete and Albert walked down Wordsworth Street. The lights were on in many of the windows and the streetlights lit the scene. They both sniffed appreciatively at the scent of liver and bacon wafting from an open window. Further on came the sounds of Bob Marley. A lighted window showed people laughing and dancing to the music.

Albert pulled on his lead. He wanted to run and catch up on the local smells. They reached the seafront, the promenade. Pete released Albert who ran off on his own concerns. Pete stood and listened to the sound of the ocean. It would be his forty-fifth birthday tomorrow. What had he done with his life? But what did his life matter in the scheme of things?

He heard a light tread on the concrete. A smiling young woman appeared from a path to the right, a trim whippet at her side. Albert woofed to greet the little dog, wagging his tail.

'Hi.' The woman addressed Pete. 'I like your dog. What's his name?'

'Albert. What's yours called?'

'Susie.'

'She looks young.'

'She's seven but she doesn't know it.'

'Albert was a rescue dog, but I think he's about five.'

The dogs chased each other, living for the moment, as dogs do.

Pete tightened his scarf. 'It's a chilly evening – I do hate these winter nights.'

'"The nights are coming now in the afternoon." I read that line in a poem by the poet Jackie Kay.'

'I'm not one for poetry'. 'Come on Albert. I need my tea now.' Goodbye then and goodbye to you Susie - good dog.'

Walking back to his flat Pete reflected that if it wasn't for Albert he wouldn't have gone out at all this evening. His job as a handyman was often outside and cold in winter, but Albert could sleep in the old van while he worked and have the occasional cuddle and treats at break time.

Opening the door into his cold flat Pete turned on his electric fire. He opened his tin of beans and, suddenly ravenous, ate them straight from the tin.

The Winter Visitor

Before Long it was Snowing Hard

2

The Winter Visitor

They walked down the lane between woods on one side and an empty field on the other. Becky could see an old cottage at the edge of the clump of bare, frosty trees. There was an untidy garden with old apple trees and wild hedges, black and spiky in the cold. Sparrows quarrelled in the bushes. The wind was getting up.

Becky, a promising photographer, was visiting her uni friend Cheryl, for the weekend. She pushed her pale blonde hair back from her face and, scrabbling in her pocket for an elastic band, pulled it into a pony tail.

'That cottage is rather spooky isn't it?' Becky rubbed her hands to keep warm.   'Do you know who lives there?'

Cheryl followed her gaze. 'There's a writer. Olivia Jackman. We used to call her the Wicked Witch of Low Woods when we were little.'

'It looks like something out of Narnia.' Becky pulled out her camera and took two or three atmospheric shots of the cottage and trees.

Cheryl coughed, impatiently stamping her feet to keep warm.

'I should never have invited you in the winter. Hanging around in the cold is not my idea of fun! The perils of having a photographer for a friend!'

She smiled to take the sting away.

'She's as grumpy as ever' thought Becky.

Olivia had been looking out of her living room window watching the goldfinches feeding on the sunflower hearts in the feeder hanging in her tree. She'd seen the two young women looking at her house. 'Just girls really. Phoebe.' She told her tabby cat. She moved the cat from her armchair and picked up her book again.

There was a desk with a laptop and printer, bookshelves filled two walls. Books overflowed from their shelves and lay in piles on the floor. There was a framed lino print of a still life with tulips, a collection of Victorian seed packets captured behind glass, and an old ordnance survey map of the local area pinned by the window.

After half an hour she began to get hungry. She walked slowly through to the kitchen and found a rather stale homity pie in the fridge. She'd have to catch the bus into Brampton this afternoon to stock up on supplies. It looked as though it might snow soon too. She missed her car but had, at last, admitted that her eyesight wasn't up to the job any longer. Anyway she might as well take advantage of her bus pass. She *was* nearly eighty.

While she was sitting at the kitchen table eating her pie she looked over at some photographs mounted together in two large frames. There were pictures of family and friends from her youth in one. The other showed pictures taken at this cottage. A baby in a buggy, one of her in her 30s, as a pretty young woman in flared jeans with a small boy,

a third, the same boy in his teens with blond hair and a bicycle. The last showed him as a handsome young man with a leather jacket. She pointed at the one of woman and child –

'That's me with Mark, my son' she told the cat. 'He must be fifty now. I haven't seen him for thirty years'

Olivia's son had disappeared thirty years ago while at college. All efforts to trace him had failed. She had no idea whether he was alive or dead. Part of her life had been on hold since 1988.

She got up to make some tea. 'It would be his birthday soon. The 21st of December.' She swallowed the lump that was in her throat...

'That's life Phoebe'. She said sadly.

*

Half a mile up the road in a modern estate Cheryl lived with her parents. There wasn't much to do in Brampton for women in their twenties.   She had agreed to go carol singing with a group of friends in support of a local hospice the next day.

'Will you come with us Becky?' It's not bad once you get started.'

'Yes – it'll be cool!'

They met up with three of Cheryl's friends in the afternoon and set out. They sang at several houses and collected quite a few pounds for the charity. Cheryl had been a supporter since they'd looked after her grandfather so well.

'Let's sing at The Wicked Witch's house.' One of Cheryl's friends suggested.

'This will be the last carol. Please! It's going to snow.' Begged Cheryl. 'I'm frozen'

*

At Olivia's house they sang *Hark the Herald Angels*. Half-way through the first verse it did begin to snow. In fact before long it was snowing hard. Olivia was watching from her kitchen window. She opened the outside door to an icy wind.

'Come in! Do!' She called through the swirling flakes. 'You'll catch your deaths.'

'Oh thank you!' Cheryl trudged in the door followed by Becky and the rest of the troupe.

'Would you like tea or whisky? How about some mince pies? Olivia had been for her Christmas supplies.

Becky was always interested in photographs and gravitated to the family ones in the two big frames. She was intrigued by these glimpses of people's lives. She peered closely at the one of the attractive young man in a leather jacket.

Everyone had drunk their tea or whisky by then and Cheryl had decided she and Becky should walk home before any more snow fell. The other three were getting a lift from a Landrover-owning parent who was a farmer.

'We need to leave now! Thank you so much Miss Jackman. That whisky was ace.'

'Do come again sometime. It's good to have company.'

*

Next morning Cheryl went back to bed after breakfast, nursing a hangover, the result of a couple more seasonal whiskies at home.

Becky knew she had to go back to Miss Jackman's house. Well muffled up, she walked back down the hill, past the wood. She saw a light on at Olivia's kitchen window. Walking up to the door she saw that the old lady had already cleared the path. Somehow this gave her courage. She knocked.

Olivia came to the door.

'Hello – Come in. Did you get home alright? How can I help you?'

'I know it's a bit of a cheek but I so wanted to see you again.' Becky shifted her feet a little.

'I've brought you some chocolates.' (She'd had them in her case for emergencies, liking to be prepared).

'Er - Thank you. Come in. To what do I owe this pleasure?'

Becky gripped her hands together. She would do this! It was too important not to!

'I wanted to ask you about one of your photos. This one.'

Becky indicated the one of the young man with blond hair. 'I've seen it before. In fact I know it well.'

'That's my son Mark, I'm afraid we aren't in touch. He disappeared thirty years ago.' Spoken with resignation.

'To me it's a photo of my father, John.'

Olivia sat down with a thump. 'Go on then!   How can this be?

'My father has the same photo. It's him as a young man.' Becky said.

'My dad was found, injured, on Snowden when he was young. He'd lost his memory. No ID. He didn't even know his name.' Becky sat down opposite Olivia.

'Please carry on!'

'The nurses at the hospital called him John. All he had was this photo in the inner pocket of his leather jacket.'

Olivia looked at the image of her beloved only child with his blond hair. Then she spoke slowly -

'I never knew what had happened to him. Searched high and low. Had the police forces of three counties looking for him, but they said he was an adult he had a free choice '

Then it really clicked.

 'Oh my Lord! You must be my granddaughter!   Is my Mark still alive?' Olivia's face fell at the thought that he might not be, even after all this new hope.'

'He's fine. We live in Cardiff. He owns a bicycle shop.

'A bicycle shop?'

'He's been married to my mother for twenty seven years. She was one of the nurses at the hospital.'

'Oh Lord! What I'd give to speak to him.'

'I'll phone him in a bit. He's always been desperate to know about his past. He sometimes seems rather sad that he doesn't know who he really was.'

Olivia didn't know whether to laugh or cry.

'Come here! Let me give you a hug. We've got a lifetime of catching up to do.'

Every Cloud

Men, Machines and Mud

3

Every Cloud

'You wouldn't believe it Becky! Ernie Watson's sold Banks Field to Bell's the builders. They're going to build twelve houses on it.'

Becky held the receiver away from her ear. Her grandmother, Olivia, was getting quite agitated.

'That's the field opposite you, where we walked three Springs ago, just after we found each other. Can't you fight it Gran? Aren't there any special wild flowers or grass snakes in the field?'

'Sadly No. I've already thought of that one!'

'You could start a petition. I'm sure a lot of the people up the road would sign it. I would and I could ask Dan to.'

Becky, originally from Wales was now teaching in Carlisle. Dan was her partner of one year.

*

Four weeks later Olivia was skyping her son John, in Cardiff.

'Well I did start a petition, I even got twenty signatures, but it wasn't enough to influence the Council's decision.'

She pushed the grey hair out of her eyes, her expression grim. 'Sadly I'm afraid the building *will* take place.'

John tried to offer hope. 'Maybe it won't be so bad.'

'They're already ripping up the hedgerows. The birds will lose their nesting sites. I don't get so many at my sunflower hearts.'

She stroked Phoebe, her cat. 'There'll be all the lorries, and then there'll be the cars. I worry about Phoebe too; she's not used to so much traffic.

*

Over the next six months the noise and disruption from across the road became more and more intrusive.

'Men, machines and mud.' Olivia informed Phoebe looking into her yellow eyes. 'Just what I wanted to get away from when I moved here all those years ago!'

Olivia, with a deadline for her detective novel looming, wasted a lot of good writing time online, looking at cottages in rural Scotland. They had to be on a bus route, which made it harder. Maybe she'd just have to move into a Home and be done with it! Maybe the End was Nigh – for her anyway.

*

Eventually the first of the new houses was finished, A For Sale board went up, viewers came and went – some just curious. The estate agent from Hedge and Heath would wave nervously at Olivia as she scowled at him whilst putting out her bird food. He'd grown up calling her The Wicked Witch of Low Wood, like all the local children, and still had an illogical whisker of belief that she could cast spells.

Then a new board announced **Sold.** An overweight young couple arrived in a white people carrier with three squalling youngsters. Then they all got out and surveyed the scene, the children squealed, the parents shouted. The father produced a key and opened the door. Ten minutes later a removal van arrived and started moving in their furniture.

Depressed, Olivia considered her options. She could learn to live with it, or she could move. The latter could be worse in all sorts of ways.

Becky phoned that evening.

'Hi Gran! I hear that the new people are starting to move in. How are you feeling?'

'All the better for hearing you! Lass. I'll just have to get used to it. I've had plenty of my own company over the years. It won't do me any harm to see some young faces about.'

'Good, I'm glad you're beginning to accept the inevitable.'

'No choice!'

'Well on a lighter note - I've got some good news! Dan and I are going to buy a house together.'

Becky and Dan had been seeing each other for over a year now and it was obviously getting serious.

'Oh wonderful. He seems a really kind young man, and so nice looking too.'

'He's ace. But that's not the only good thing. We've looked at one in the new estate opposite you, we've got a mortgage arranged, and our offer's been accepted. We should be able to move in six weeks or so.'

'Oh lovely Dear. You've certainly kept that a secret. Would you like to come over for tea and a cake sometime to chat about it?'

*

Eight weeks later Olivia was drinking a glass of Merlot with Becky and Dan after a roast chicken cooked by Dan in their new home.

'Well! It's lovely to have you so near. Your plans for wildlife in your garden, pond and all sound just so hopeful. Maybe every cloud really does have a silver lining.'

Pot Luck

The Spanish Cat

4
Pot Luck

Lucy spent every spare minute scouring charity shops. She was searching for just one item. She looked in vintage shops, junk shops, online at Etsy and eBay. She had a regular date with Antiques Road Show.

She couldn't find it and its loss was gnawing at her.

She was losing confidence, turning from a bright positive twenty-year-old to a scared, negative twenty one-year-old.

*

It was a small piece of Spanish pottery, a 1950s bud vase, a stylised and decorative cat. Lucy's grandmother had always kept it on a white shelf unit along with her books.

Sixteen-year-old Lucy had loved the china feline and Gran had noticed.

'Would you like the Spanish cat Lucy dear? Here! It's yours! It will bring you good luck.'

'Oh thank you Gran!' She gave her Gran a big hug.

*

Four years later Lucy had left home to start a new job in the city. She had moved into a shared house. She had a new boyfriend.

One day Lucy forgot to lock the front door. There was a robbery at the house. The Spanish vase was missing, along with the television, and Lucy's pot of two pound coins saved for a holiday in Barcelona. They got the old TV back but not the money or the lucky vase.

Lucy was made redundant. Her boyfriend ditched her.

She became obsessed about the loss of her Gran's gift.

'My Luck has gone.' She said to Trudie, her house mate.

*

Lucy spoke to her witchy Aunt Gwen about her search. Her aunt was known to have special powers.

'I've got a drawing of that vase. I loved it too.' Aunt Gwen realised. 'Maybe you'd like that. I'll bless it with an extra special good luck spell.'

Lucy was cheered by her aunt's drawing. The next day she framed and hung it. As she relaxed, listening to music that evening, the cats in the picture seemed to be grinning at her. She smiled back, thinking of her gran's original present of the bud vase.

*

Two days later she received a letter offering her a position as assistant manager of one of the classier Antique Shops in town. It was one she'd often visited during her search for the Spanish Cat Vase. Tom, the owner was impressed by her interest in pottery and in remembered objects.

A Bit of a Struggle

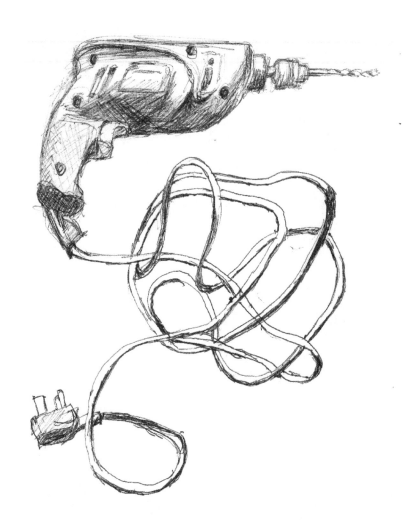

I didn't have the right Drill Bit

5

A Bit of a Struggle

I can hear the wind strong in the trees - the clock ticking –
the sound of a drill in short bursts from outside. The dog is
moving, getting comfortable on her chair. The metal
screams again – the door squeaks open and bangs shut.

These noises have been continuing intermittently for half
an hour. No words have been spoken.

'I'm not fighting on with this!' David exclaims.

 Mechanical screaming again. Small piece of metal tings on
concrete. Wind wailing – short drill-burst. Rush of wind
into the house. A plug is pulled out. Click of chuck key
against metal.

'I can't do it! It's not much of a thing if it doesn't do it. The
drill bit broke.'

There is a crash – slam – footsteps across the room.
Sounds of small pieces of metal clinking in a tin.

'I've found some more drill bits. I'll try once more – this is a
new one.'

 A longer burst of metal screeching against stone – Doors
open and close –

I speak for the first time 'How did it go?'

'Well I've got one hole made. I want to see the other one's
in the right place before I do that.'

Three more trips to and from the kitchen and slight sounds
of aggravation.

Back outside the torture starts again for five short bursts, then a longer one, three more short, and two longer, louder blasts. Click, click.

Spoken under his breath - 'That'll do! Give it the works James. Give it the works.'

Long, loud burr of noise, clink of metal – sigh –

'Check again! Spot on! See if it goes in.'

Hammering of rubber. David enters the house.

'Done it?'

'No not yet dear'

Steps across the room – back door – steps across room, front door - grunt

More drilling - it is loud and long - screaming and juddering. Stops then starts again. Stops – clink - starts again jarring my teeth - changes note to a slower, lower sound, then high short bursts, tails off, clink.

Back and forth across the room.

The dog licks her lips, jumps off her chair, walks around a bit, jumps back on her chair, looks at me and gets settled again.

Doors open and close. Slam!

The dog gets up and walks around. David walks across the room again and goes out the front. The dog opens and closes her mouth.

There is the whoosh of strong wind in the tree in the front garden. I sigh. The dog gets off her chair and comes to me for a cuddle.

'Are you alright girl?'

A wood pigeon coos. There are slight metallic noises. The wind is loud. Silence.

 David enters the room.

'Well I've done it! The machine really wasn't up to the job and the brick was stone hard - but I've done it!'

'Well done!! You don't give up do you? How about a cup of tea?'

Entertainment in Lockdown

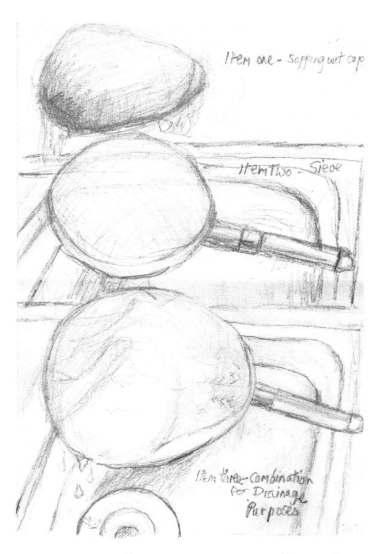

Item one - Sopping wet cap

Item Two - Sieve

Item three - Combination for Drainage Purposes

Turning the Sieve over solves the Problem

6

Entertainment in Lockdown

David - Do you think you could clean my old cap? I don't want to start on my new one. There's life in the old one yet.

Barbara - I don't see why not. I'll see what I can do – I'll Google it!

*

I Google - HOW TO CLEAN A MEN'S FLAT CAP UK.

I find amongst others, a website entitled Trendhim, featuring a fashionable looking man with a full grey moustache and beard, black eyebrows and photos of him wearing various tasteful flat caps, designed by Moda, hand made in Italy, obviously the height of fashion. I don't think this is quite what I was looking for.

What's this? HOW TO WASH A BRITISH WOOL FLAT CAP.

1 – Fill a sink with lukewarm water, add a small amount of Woolite or other wool washing liquid.

2 – Soak the cap for 5-7 minutes – rub the peak lightly with a soft, clean towel to clean.

3 – Rinse well

4 – Pat with clean dry towel to soak up water.

5 - Air dry.

At this point I return my half-sister's missed phone call.

Jane -   Hello Barbara.

Barbara -   Hello Jane. How's it going?

Jane -   Well – the usual - grey skies - imprisoned here. I'll go out to get my prescription if it cheers up. I can't contain my excitement. How's it in Scotland?

Barbara -   It's very wild and windy. I don't think I'll get out today.

J -   What have you been doing with yourself?

B -   I think I told you we were doing an online writing course?

J -   Yes. I did a creative writing course once. Is that what you mean? I wrote a poem about my mother when I was five. (She repeats it from memory. It's not very complimentary.)

B -   Yes that's the kind of thing. We have an impossible task this time – To write something funny. I've got absolutely no idea where to start.

J - Yes - I can see what you mean. What are you going to do this afternoon?

B - Well – I'm going to wash David's flat cap. I looked it up online.

J - You could write about that. Maybe the cat could get the cap and run away with it.

B – I suppose I could. That's certainly as good as any idea I've come up with.

*

I fill a sink with water, add a little washing liquid for wool, leave it to soak, rub it lightly with a soft towel, rinse it well and I'm left with a problem not mentioned in the article online - but one I had anticipated. How to get rid of the water.

I take our kitchen sieve, prop it side to side over the sink put the cap in it to drain. David comes along to see what I am doing and comes up with a better, revised solution – turns the sieve over and treats it like a head to place the cap on. It fits perfectly and solves the problem.

I leave the cap in position for an hour or two, meanwhile attempting to draw the combination. The drawing doesn't quite come off, but I think I may be able to do a further explanatory drawing of the two components.

When most of the water has drained off - I mop up the rest with a clean dry towel.

I then place it on a clothes-drying rack to air dry. This takes a couple of days and the cap is returned to its owner – good as new. Another money saving idea!

One week later

There is one unanticipated aftermath of the afternoon recorded above. For the last week I have, each time I opened Google or my email page, been bombarded with images of bearded men of all ages in flat caps, courtesy of the website of Trendhim.

Food from the Platter

Dot carrying the Platter of
Sandwiches

7

Food from the Platter

South West Scotland 2021

I am about to serve dinner. We are having Diana Henry's cumin-roast aubergines, chickpeas. walnuts and dates. I will serve it on my grandmother's meat platter. Nellie's platter is Royal Doulton earthenware, blue on white, with a pattern of leaves and flowers. There are a few dinners we use this platter for. Another is Moroccan Tuna Nicoise from a book called Postcards from Marrakesh.

In our present house in south west Scotland the platter lives on a shelf above the fridge-freezer, but inside the built-in door for that appliance. The shelf is rather high for me to reach, and the platter weighs 2.5 Kilos. I have to concentrate each time I take it out or put it back in. A smaller, newer, Masons Ironstone platter rests on top of it which needs to be put in separately.

The Royal Doulton platter, along with vegetable dishes, with or without covers, dinner plates and a gravy boat lived in my mother, Dot's built-in cupboard, in her house in Essex. The cupboard was on the right of her coal fire, the bottom cupboard being used for newspapers for lighting the fire. The blue and white earthenware had been in the same display for as long as I remembered, back to my grandmother's day and my young childhood.

The platter is much too large for regular use as a meat platter. Maybe that was why it has remained intact.

I wondered if the set had been a wedding present for my grandparents, married in 1912, or had it originally belonged to Nanna's mother, Fanny Perry? When I looked into how old it was, I found that this pattern was first made in 1927 which put the kybosh on those theories.

*

St Mary's Church in Dunmow, Essex 1952

The bellringers are hosts to the ringers from Wimbish. Alf Wiffen is Wimbish Tower Captain and Walter Smith bears that office at St Mary's. The Wimbish ringers are joining Walter's team in a quarter peal of Plain Bob Major. The work is hard and demands utmost concentration. The whole team is sweating. There are eight bells, and the quarter peel will take six hours in all.

Dot, Walter's daughter rings the treble for an hour, then George Blower takes her place. Dot rides her bicycle home to help her mother Nellie prepare the tea for the ringers. Nellie has been busy since early morning baking – cherry cakes, Victoria sponges, scones. All the Dunmow ringers' families have contributed from their rations of sugar, eggs, butter and marge for this occasion.

Dot weighs in, slicing bread, very thinly and buttering it – washing celery and trimming it into sticks, slicing cucumber. She hard boils eggs. When they are cold she mashes them with a trace of salad cream. She slices spam. She fills sandwiches and arranges them on her mother's big blue and white platter.

At last the feast is prepared. The flaps are pulled out of the front room table. The chairs are pulled out to the side of the room. The best tablecloth is on the table. (A felt cloth is underneath for protection.) The sandwiches and huffers are cut and displayed on the blue and white platter. Plates covered with doilies are filled with cakes and scones, and there are piles of side plates with paper serviettes.

Dot keeps on looking out of the window to see if the ringers are on their way. She has heard the ringing winding down towards the end. The quarter peal has been completed successfully.

After twenty minutes she sees her father Walter and Alf Wiffen leading the ringers as fast as their weary legs will carry them through the gate in the hawthorn hedge across the road. They have walked across the Rec from the church and are all hungry and thirsty. Dot opens the stiff, rarely-used front door with some effort.

There is much welcoming and congratulating. Nellie has already started pouring tea into the lined up cups.

Alf Wiffen's son Lew is there with his fiancée. She needs the toilet and is taken through the kitchen, the scullery and the back yard to the outside lavatory. Two small girls are playing in the yard, me Dot's daughter, and my friend Margaret. Lew's fiancée smiles and waves at us.

*

2009 St Mary's Church, Dunmow.

The memorial service for Dot Goodhew nee Smith has just finished and tea and sandwiches are being served by Dot's much younger friend Rosemary. I, Dot's daughter, am mingling with the crowd.

An old man introduces himself as Lew Wiffen. I remember the name very well as a noted ringer.

46

'Your mother Dot was a stalwart of the ringers.' He says.

'We used to have tea at your grandparents, my wife and me. Your grandmother was famous for her teas, and your grandfather was a fine ringer. We all used to look forward to ringing at St Mary's.

Lew finishes by saying that he remembers me as a child playing in the yard.

'Oh - I well remember your name Mr Wiffen. You were often spoken of at home, regarding peals you had rung. Do have some of these sandwiches, Rosemary made them – she used to ring. This platter was my grandmother's. She used to serve sandwiches on it sometimes. I expect you may have had some from it before in the dim, distant past.'

Just Another Morning

8

JUST ANOTHER MORNING

It was two weeks since Andy and Sue had stopped drinking.

There was some hope. Now they could get on track for the first time. They couldn't afford to go to the pub every night that was for sure. There was only her money coming in.

Andy had walked out of the glue factory after another argument with the boss. Well! Sue admitted, he was certainly beginning to smell less pungent now.

She remembered when she and Andy had travelled for an interview for jobs as live-in housekeeper and odd job man in Kent. They had hitched through the driving rain. Exhausted, they had tried to get some rest in a ditch by the motorway – soaked and numb with cold.

They had not been accepted for this employment.

Now Andy called through from the bedroom –

'What's for breakfast?'

'Tea and toast'

They ate their toast and then he switched on the television and sat staring at the breakfast programmes. Sue washed up and started to do some ironing. Time passed until a quarter to eleven.

'I think I'll go for a pint at the Duke's Arms'

'But we haven't got any money left!'

'Well I've got a couple of quid I found.'

'We're not supposed to be drinking. It's our only chance of paying the bills.'

'I'll only stay for one. ..... You don't mind do you?'

Andy took off his dark glasses and gave Sue the blue-eyed smile he still thought was so appealing. He put on his tan leather jacket, grabbed his keys and walked out of the door.

Sue paced round the kitchen and cursed with frustration and defeat. She'd had enough – but she was committed, married. She felt trapped, as though she was struggling up a hill of mud and was continually falling back to the bottom.

She decided to phone her older friend Sheila – a woman of sixty five who she'd known for years from The Market Tavern, her old local in Keswick.

'Hello Sheila – how are you doing?'

'Alright. It's cold isn't it? I think there'll be snow. How's Andy?'

'Well – He's just gone down the pub.'

'I thought you'd given up the booze.'

He found some money somewhere.'

'You should leave him you know!'

'You've not said anything before.'

'But you must have known what I thought.'

Sue had wrestled with the pros and cons of leaving Andy through many a dark night.

'I've no money and it's too hard to plan.'

Your brother would lend you some if it was to get away, you've got the car now. Come down to me. I'll expect you. I'll make up the spare room.

'I can't do that! How would he manage?'

'He managed before he got you in this situation! Well I'll expect you. If you don't get away from that man now you can whistle for my support.'

'Well – you know I might just do that – I may see you later.'

Sue thought of the possibility of a life without constant alarms and excursions - one where you could plan your finances, pay bills as they fell due and not have to keep moving, leaving rent, bar tabs and loans unpaid.

She was excited at the thought of living her own life but scared too. It was five years since she's been on her own. Change was always frightening, and she'd burnt her bridges for the old life before Andy.

Also she felt guilty. He depended on her so much – saying she'd have to look after him in his old age. Not something she fancied – he was hard enough to deal with now.

She was in a quandary, struggling, in high emotion.

She decided to go – she gathered handbag, purse, passport, driving licence, a few clothes and toiletries. She left Andy her address book in case he needed telephone numbers, wrote a note saying she was leaving – good luck for the future - and walked out of the door.

She went to her brother and borrowed some money. She said her brother should know nothing when Andy inevitably called.

Driving towards the Lake District she was scared Andy was following - though how this was possible when he didn't drive or know where she was going she didn't know.

She drove with the music turned up high - *her* choice of music not Andy's.

'On the Road Again'

Over the Top

Over the Top

9

Over the Top

Mike poured the last of the strong cider down his hardened throat – tasted the bile that bubbled up from his belly to meet it - smelt the stale urine and beer from his torn jeans. He passed the empty to his mate Jeff, climbed into the roller coaster car and wondered why he'd let Jeff talk him into choosing a fairground ride for his birthday treat. Forty-nine. Near the end for a street liver – scarred liver – cirrhosis.

The car climbed steadily to the summit, then sped down the other side. The sky went hazy and Mike's brain felt as though it was exploding. Red and yellow lights.

*

Then he finds himself in the calm of an early October day. – autumnal smells. His head clear and free – his body strong and well. An unfamiliar feeling in his gut – Happiness?? He smiles.

He feels a small hand nudge his arm.

"Dad look! You can see the sheep on the hill over there." A child's face – brown eyes like Sam's. His son Sam.

But – what about that day twenty years ago? When there was the screech of brakes – keening wife – small still body. Sam, never to be more than five years old.

In the Picture

10

In the Picture

At the top of the stairs in our small modern semi, is an etching by Richard Bawden depicting the staircase of a tall Victorian house. The hallway shows a checkerboard of tiles. There is a cat, or the ghost of a cat running full pelt down the stairs, its feet not touching the treads. The crosshatch shading is rather mysterious, even spooky, the drawing precise and spirited.

My story started when I was doing an exercise for a healthy heart. I walked up and down our stairs five times consecutively, each day. I religiously kept it up for a week, the last climb being quite strenuous. I managed a fortnight gradually increasing, until, by the end of the month I was doing ten times. Although I was getting fitter, it was still a struggle by the end of the session. Focussing on the picture at the top of the stairs gave me encouragement.

On that particular day I started on the eleventh time, reached the landing, and, concentrating, as usual on our etching I struggled into the picture, over that checkerboard of tiles, and up those stairs. I found myself in a grey world, in a misty half-light. A tabby cat raced past me, heading down.

When I'd laboured up this further flight I slumped over and regained my breath for a couple of minutes. I heard the cat yowling at the bottom of the stairs.

Through a slightly open door on the other side of the landing I heard strains of Bessie Smith singing *Ain't Nobody's Business if I do.* I pushed the door open and found myself in a large room flooded with light from a window nearly the width of the room. There were framed prints on one wall. An etching press filled the side of the room, with a rack full of drying prints nearby. I'd found the Artist's studio. As I looked on, a tall, stooped man with white hair and beard entered through another door. He looked at me with surprise.

'Hello - who are you? I wasn't expecting any visitors.'

'My name's Barbara and it's very strange but I walked into one of your etchings'

'Hmm!??? !!!!! - - - - - Which one?'

'Well, it's called "In Pursuit" but I think the cat's being chased, not chasing.'

'Well that's your prerogative I suppose. So – where did you see my etching?

'My husband, David and I bought it last year.'

'Where did you buy it?'

'The Bircham Gallery in Holt.   Could I possibly have a look at some of your work? I'm a great fan.'

He smiled and ushered me over to the wall filled with framed work. He indicated a wonderfully detailed misty blue etching of a garden with mature winter trees seen through a large window. On the window sill were an antique wine glass, a bowl of red and yellow tulips and a brown and black striped cat looking out. Coming up the path across a large lawn was a yellow tabby cat. 'This is called Welcome Home.'

'Oh! I love it! I've seen it in the book 'The Printmaker's Cat' and really it's my favourite.'

'You seem to know my work pretty well. How come?

'I was at Colchester Art School in 1966 and was supposed to come to your Printmaking classes on Friday afternoons. I'm afraid I used to hitch home to my mother instead.'

'Students! Most of you don't deserve to succeed! You missed out by not doing Printmaking you know.'

'But I did do it later. I did several series of evening classes, etching, aquatint, and screen printing.'

'I suppose you want to show me your work!

'I could bring something if I can get back in.'

'Fine – If you can.'

I said goodbye, thanks and I'd hope to see him again. Out to the landing, and, in a moment of exhilaration I decided to slide down the banisters. I slid straight down to our landing.

David came out of his office – 'Do you want a cup of tea? I heard you doing your stairs exercises earlier – How many did you do today?'

'I did ten. Then – something very peculiar happened. I walked straight into our 'In Pursuit' picture. I've been talking to Richard Bawden for half an hour.'

'You're barking! You've finally lost it!'

'I should have known you wouldn't believe it but I know what happened!'

I sniffed a bit then went into my workroom.

60

I searched under the bed for my A1 portfolio with the plastic wallets. I found what I was looking for.

How was I to get into the picture now? I stared at 'In Pursuit' and imagined climbing into that other house. No joy. I did a further five turns at my stair-climbing exercise. Still no success.

I decided to start the dinner and think about it later. Maybe if I forgot about it, like a crossword clue, it would come to me in the morning.

Life went on. I felt inspired to draw and started a phase of not only seeing pictures and shapes but actually getting them down on paper. David was pleased to see me come fully alive.

A month into this renewed activity I was turning the pages of 'The Printmaker's Cat' in my workroom, then admiring 'Welcome Home' that had been in Richard's studio. I was on a real high because of my feverish application to my artwork. I heard a voice behind me. 'Hello'

I turned and there I was with Richard in his studio. In my hand was the print I had found to show him. I held it up.

'Moon Madcap' he read. 'Well, you know that isn't at all bad. And so appropriate!

Moon Madcap A/P   Barbara Dale

Moon Madcap

'An impish sprite harlequin-clad in jester's garb,
Mischievous creature cavorting in silver light.'

Quoted from poem by Jean Blemings

The Rockcliffe Driftwood

The Rockcliffe Driftwood in 2012

11

The Rockcliffe Driftwood

2007 Rockcliffe Cumbria

We went to Rockcliffe on the Eden estuary in Cumbria to find a large piece of driftwood. We wanted a feature for our garden in Carlisle. Some months previously we had found a small piece that reminded me of a fish or a bird. I had made several pencil studies of it. After walking over the wild, rather bleak beach, we found part of a water-worn tree. This seemed just what we were looking for and we dragged it to the car.

Back home we found a place for our driftwood in the garden. As expected, it made an interesting sculptural form. Our kitten Lizzie loved to use it as a scratching post.

2021 South West Scotland

The tree stump has moved with us to our new home and garden in Castle Douglas. It is a part of the structure that helped our now senior cat Lizzie to feel so much at home from the first.

We sometimes wonder about the journey taken by our river-borne find. What kind of tree was it a part of? Where did it start its life? How old is it?

Rockcliffe is situated on the estuary of the River Eden – not far from its outflow to the Solway Firth. Our sculpture could have been borne by flood waters from along the Eden flowing from the heights of Mallerstang, through Kirkby Stephen, Carlisle to the Solway Firth. Or the Eden being tidal, it could have come from somewhere else on the Solway Firth, from Maryport say - or Whitehaven.

Maybe it came from The River Esk which starts up in the high ground north west of Langholm and flows into the Solway Firth just south of Gretna a few miles from the Eden estuary, before being swept up the Eden by the tide.

I like to think that its birthplace was the Loch of Urr from which the River Urr flows. Sometimes called the Water of Urr it flows through Dalbeattie, home of our new Scottish allotment to enter the Solway Firth at the Scottish Rockcliffe.

Acknowledgements

Thank you to the people who ensured I complete this project.

My husband David encouraged me to continue when I would have said 'Forget it'. He advised on the publishing process, gave suggestions, particularly for titles, and endlessly chivied me on.

Jean Blemings decided me to try illustration in the 1990s and she gave permission to quote from her poem.

Vicki Bertram's workshops were a revelation, and she was a great support to us all. There is no chance I would have done this without her classes.

My thanks to members of the group – Sarah Kirkup, Clare Hallam, Dick Capel, Karen Babayan, Sue Haywood, David Haigh, Janet Price, Helen Murray and others. All gave valuable feedback and suggestions.

Richard Bawden kindly read the story in which he featured and gave permission for me to publish it. The Bircham Gallery in Holt having passed it on for me.

David's daughters, Rachel Haigh and Laura Roberts read the stories and gave good feedback. Laura also providing useful photos of diggers.

Friends helped. Jane Chittenden has always boosted my confidence re my drawing and made a helpful presentation suggestion, Caroline Ireland gave much encouragement and Rosemary Saines read the story of which she was a part and gave feedback.

Printed in Great Britain
by Amazon

83913207R00041